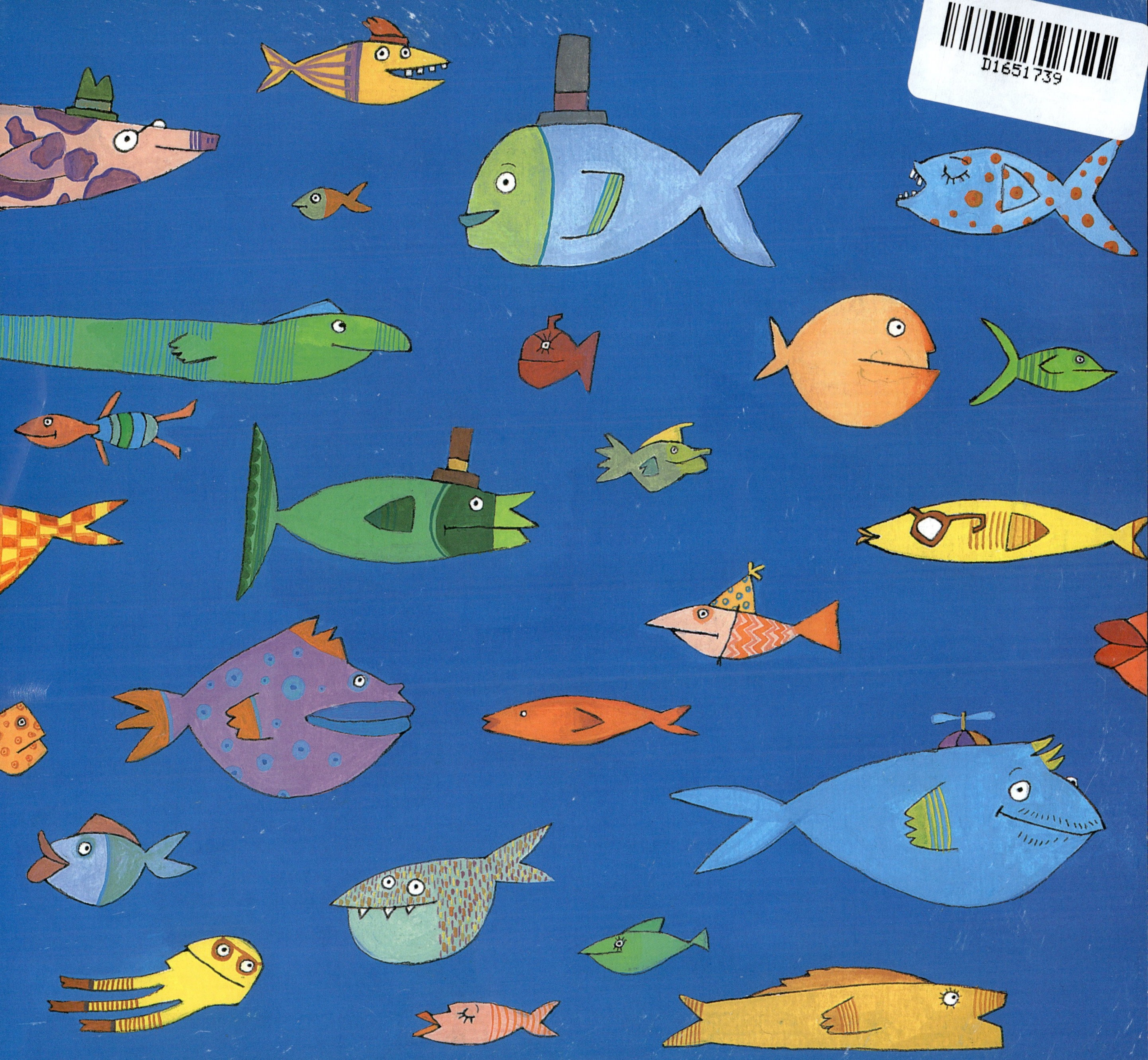

For Emma ~ A.M.

For Wayra ~ G.R.

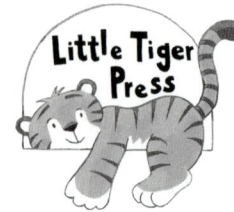

LITTLE TIGER PRESS
An imprint of Magi Publications
22 Manchester Street, London W1M 5PG

First published in Great Britain 1999

Text © 1999 Alan MacDonald

Illustrations © 1999 Glummie Riday

Alan MacDonald and Glummie Riday have asserted their
rights to be identified as the author and illustrator of this
work under the Copyright, Designs and Patents Act, 1988.

Printed in Belgium by Proost NV, Turnhout

ISBN 1 85430 492 5

1 3 5 7 9 10 8 6 4 2

A FISH FOR SUPPER

Alan MacDonald and Glummie Riday

It was a perfect day for fishing.
The sun was shining,
the breeze was blowing and
the boat bobbed merrily on the sea.
Mulligan and Starbuck were trying
to catch a fish for their supper.

"I'm going to catch a fish bigger than my boots," boasted Mulligan.

"*You?*" scoffed Starbuck. "You couldn't catch a bus."

"And *you* couldn't catch a flea," replied Mulligan, sticking out his tongue rudely.

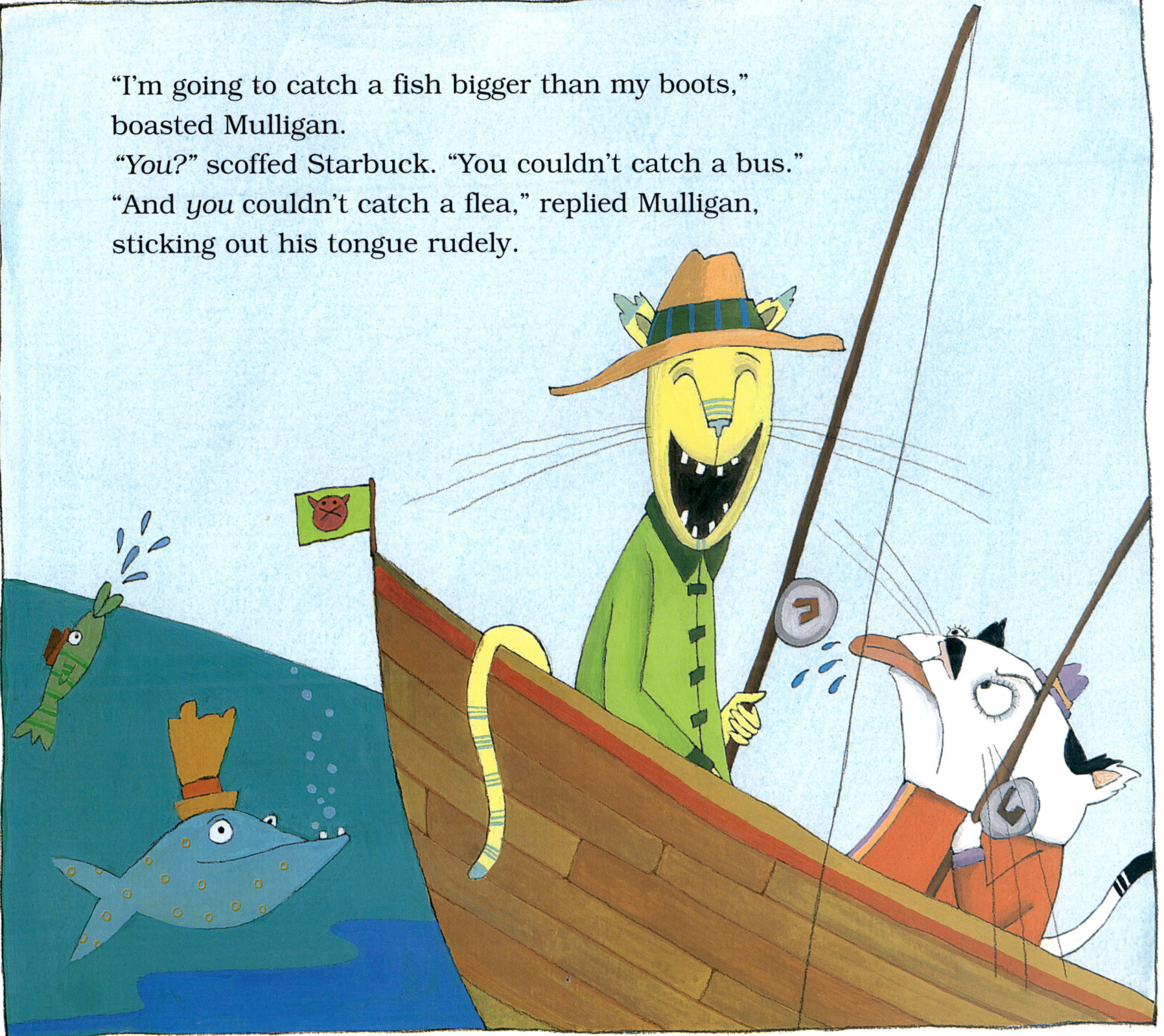

Hours passed. A cloud drifted across
the sun and a friendly seal swam by
to see who was snoring.
Mulligan and Starbuck had fallen asleep!

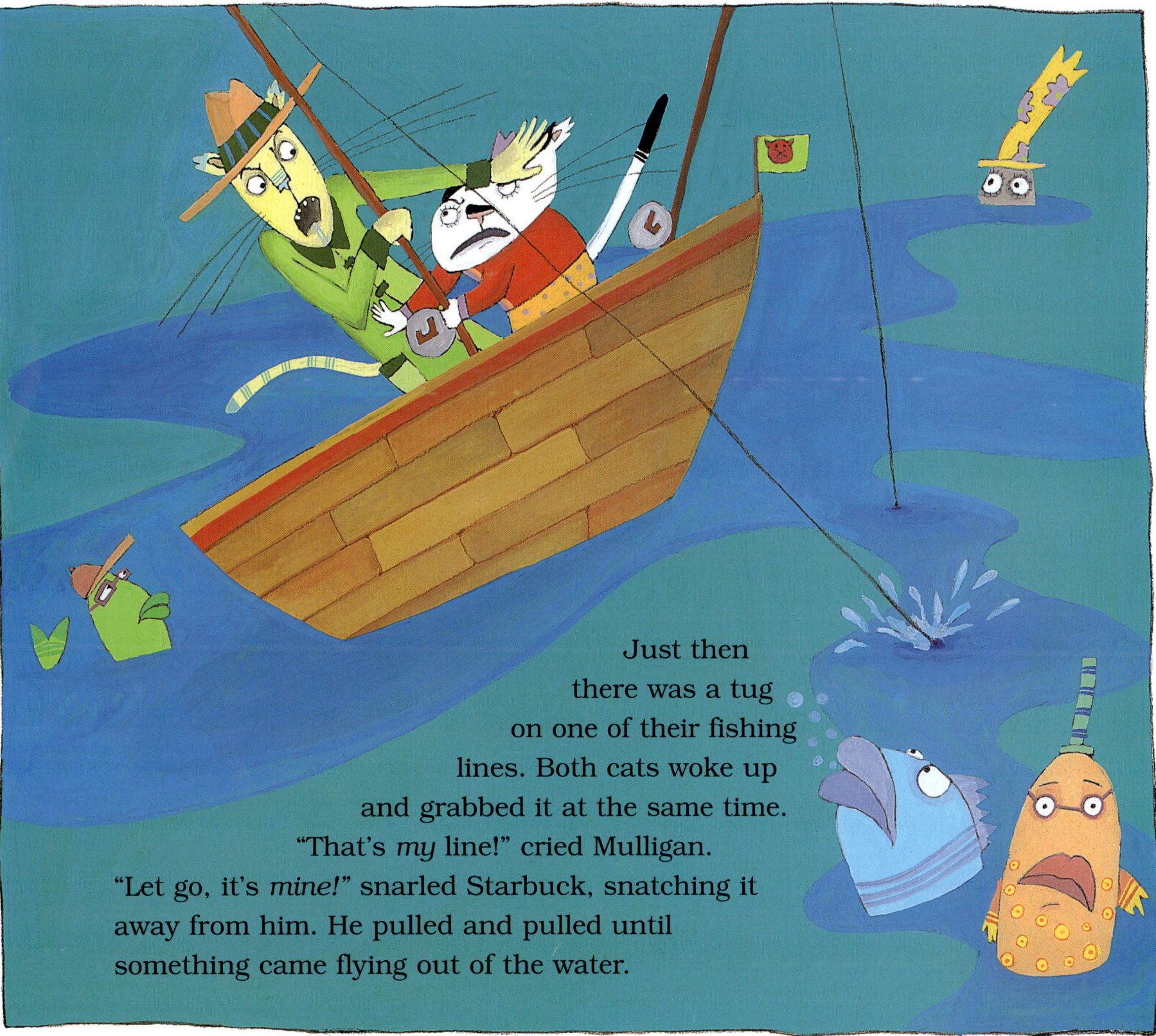

Just then
there was a tug
on one of their fishing
lines. Both cats woke up
and grabbed it at the same time.
"That's *my* line!" cried Mulligan.
"Let go, it's *mine!*" snarled Starbuck, snatching it
away from him. He pulled and pulled until
something came flying out of the water.

Dangling on the end of the line was a
huge plug on a chain!
Mulligan fell about laughing.
"Ha, ha! Try again, Starbuck.
Maybe next time you'll catch a bath!"

Starbuck glared.

He was just wondering what a plug was doing in the sea when a loud "gurgle-urgle-urgle" came from the depths of the ocean.

"We're sinking!" cried Starbuck.

"No, we're not, it's the *sea* that's sinking," said Mulligan.

Sure enough, all around them the water was going down . . .

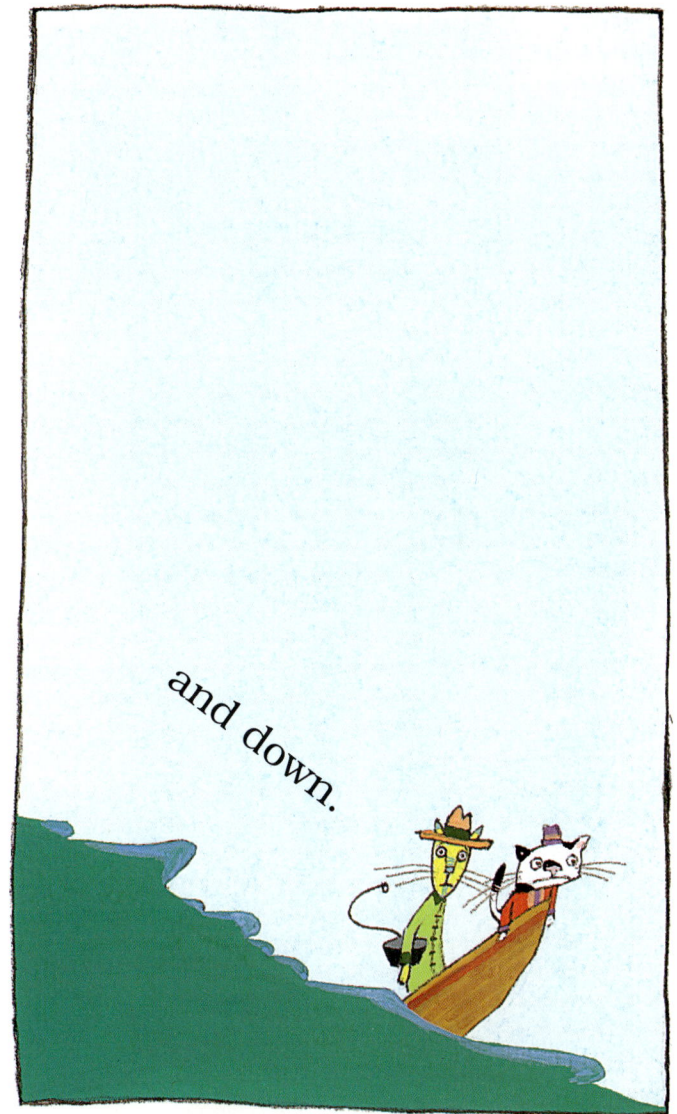

and down . . .

and down.

With a gloop, a shloop and a glug,
the sea was sucked away,
bit by bit.

HOTEL NEPTUNE

LOBSTER RETREAT

Mulligan and Starbuck got out of the boat and started
looking for the plughole in the seabed.
A group of sea creatures followed behind them,
led by an angry seal, honking crossly,
because she had nowhere to swim.

PLUG
HOLE

At last Mulligan found the hole and replaced the Plug.
Too late! There was no sea left.
"Well, Mulligan, how are you going
to bring the sea back?" asked Starbuck.
"Don't ask me, *you're* supposed to be the
clever one," sneered Mulligan.

Just then there was a
rumble of thunder . . .

PLUG HOLE
Keep away from fishing cats.

and the rain began to fall in buckets. Lightning flashed and the rain fell in rivers. In no time at all, the sea started to rise again.

"Help!" shouted Starbuck. "I've got to get back to the boat."

"Me first," said Mulligan, grabbing hold
of Starbuck.
"Let go!" snarled Starbuck.
"No, *you* let go!"
As they squabbled and fought, their boat drifted away.
Suddenly, Mulligan realised he was up to his
whiskers in water.

"Save me!" spluttered Mulligan. "I'm sinking!"
"No, save *me*," cried Starbuck. "I can't swim!"
"But I can," said the seal, as she
bobbed up between them.
"Hang on to me, and I'll tow you
to safety."

She swam with them to the boat,
and the two half-drowned cats
clambered aboard.

The sun was going down when Starbuck and Mulligan finally reached home. Their fishing rods were lost, their clothes dripping wet, and they hadn't caught a single fish for supper.

"It's all your fault!" grumbled Mulligan. "If you hadn't pulled that plug out –"

"I like that!" snapped Starbuck. "It was *your* idea to go fishing in the first place!"

The two cats went indoors and
Starbuck pulled off his boot.
Out came a puddle of water . . .

and a small silver fish!
Both cats grabbed hold of the fish at the same time.
Each held on, and wouldn't let go.
"*I* saw it first!" cried Mulligan.
"Paws off! It was in *my* boots!"
hissed Starbuck.

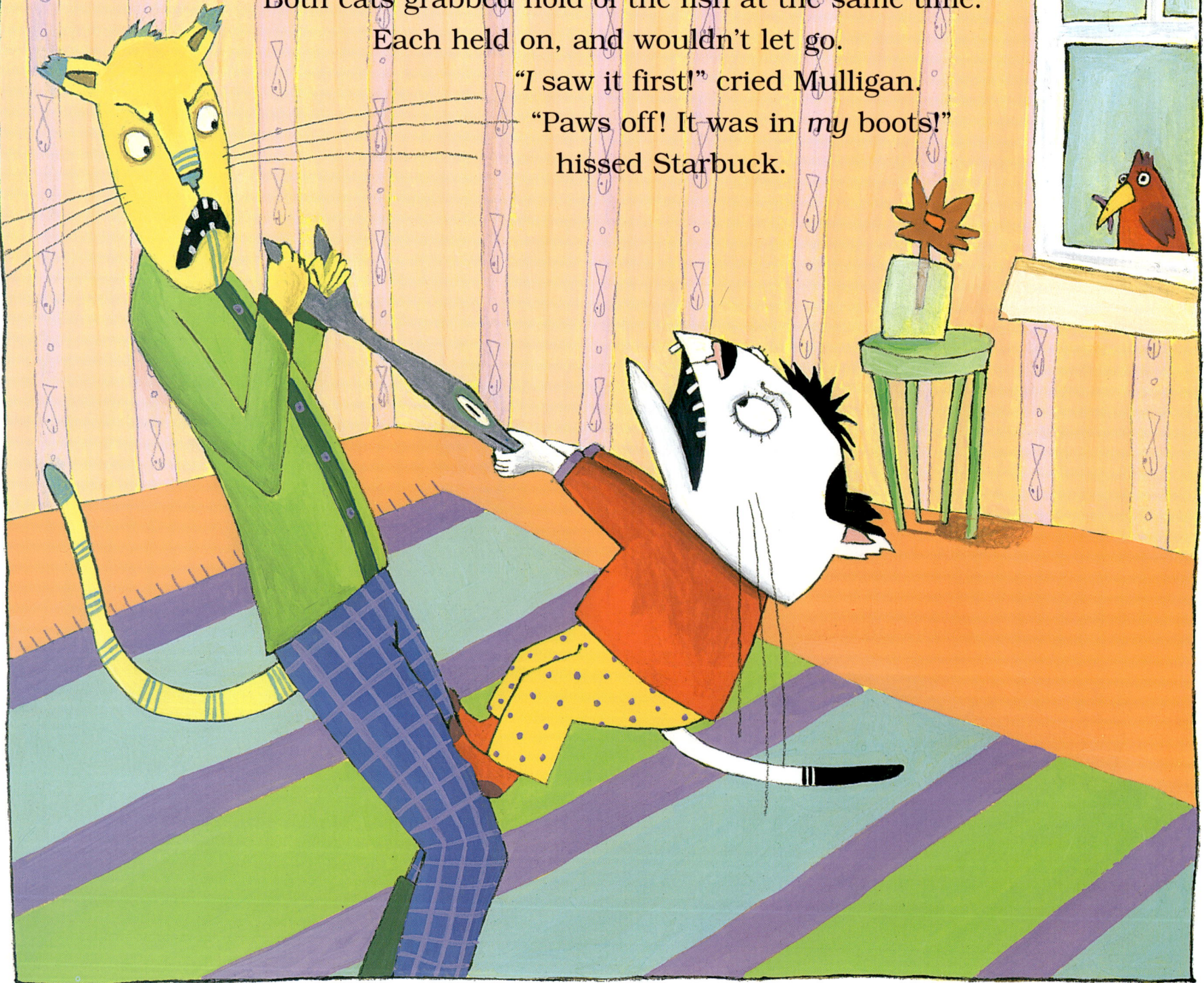

They pulled and pulled. They heaved and tugged until suddenly the slippery fish shot from their paws . . .

and flew out through the kitchen window.
Mulligan and Starbuck looked outside.
There was the seal . . .

but where was
their fish?

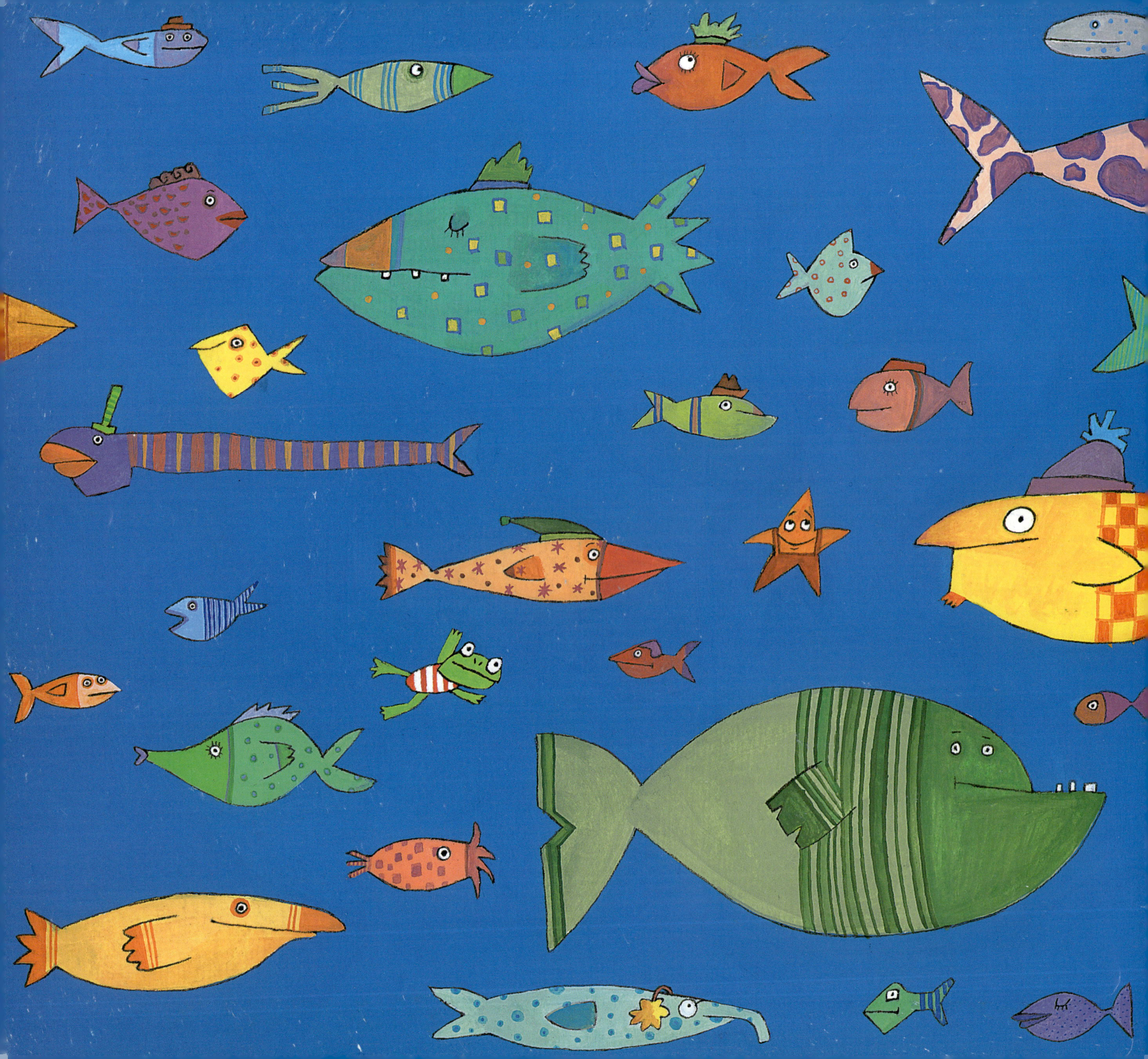